for *Tai & Ela.*

Troll Carnival
The Old Surgery
Napier Street
Cardigan
SA43 1ED
www.trollcarnival.co.uk

First published in 2009

Text: © Lewis Davies
Illustration: © Hayley Acreman

ISBN: 978 1 905762 64 4

Design: www.theundercard.co.uk

British Library Cataloguing in Publication Data
A catalogue record of this book is available from the British Library

Printed & bound by **Gwasg Gomer**, Llandysul, Wales

TROLL CARNIVAL
WWW.TROLLCARNIVAL.CO.UK

TAI, TROLL
and the
BLACK & WHITE COW

by Lewis Davies

Illustrated by Hayley Acreman

Tai was waiting patiently with his yellow rucksack and green hat.
The Troll had been a long time mumbling and muttering to himself.

'Are you ready yet?' asked Tai. '**No,**' replied the Troll.

Tai took another biscuit from his rucksack.
The Troll had promised to take Tai on a day-trip to Brecon.
The Troll had an Aunt who lived in Brecon. She sold herbs
in the market that opened every Friday.

Eventually the Troll had checked the oil, the water, the spare
tyre and the battery in the car. He sat in the driver's seat.

'**Right, we can go now,**' announced the Troll.

Tai kicked the tyre of the car.
It didn't start the first time
but on the second kick it did.

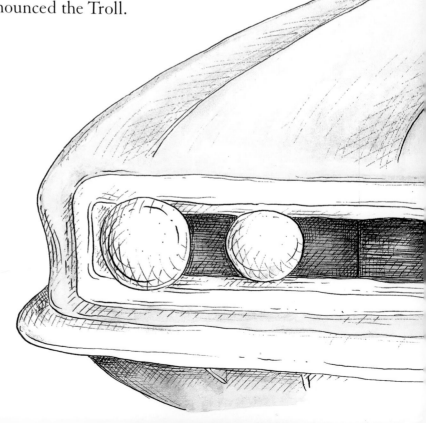

Brecon was a long way
from Tremorfa.

They had to drive over
a big mountain called
Pen-y-Fan.

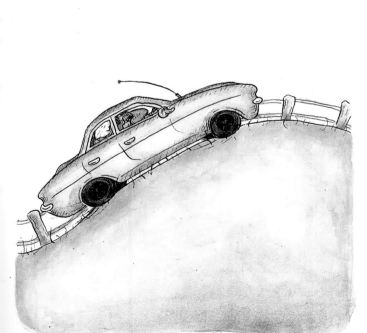

It was so high there was
snow on the top.

The old car struggled with
the hills, but once over the
top of the mountain…

...it sped down the road and went so fast the fields and hedges just flashed past and they even overtook a tractor.

Brecon was a much smaller town than Tai had imagined. It sat on a hill above the river looking rather pleased with itself and its view of the mountains.

The Troll stopped the car on the bridge to see if his Aunt was home. He leaned right over and shouted but he only scared a pair of swans and a fisherman.

They got back into the car and drove to the market. The market was not as Tai had expected. It was hidden behind a wall and Tai could hear strange noises from the far side.

HALL

FARMERS MARKET
EVERY FRIDAY

EXIT

Tai followed the Troll to a sign that said '**Auction**'. **'I think she'll be in here,'** said the Troll.

AUCTION

The auction room was in a round building, crowded with people who wore Wellingtons and green coats. The Troll with his red waistcoat and Panama hat stood out like his red nose.

In the centre of the room was a ring filled with straw and surrounded by a fence. A man standing on a box began shouting at people through a microphone. He announced **lot 29**.

'Are you sure your Aunt works in the market?'
asked Tai. The Troll looked around.
**'Can you see an old woman with
red hair selling plants?'**
Tai looked around. He could see a lot of men.
They were all wearing flat caps.

Lot 29 was a black and white cow. The cow was
pushed into the ring. The cow looked around.
The man began shouting on his microphone and
the men in hats began putting their arms in the air.

'What are they doing?' asked Tai.

'They're buying the cow,' replied the Troll.

'Can we buy a cow?' asked Tai.

The Troll looked down at Tai. **'What do you want a cow for?'**

'A souvenir,' replied Tai.

'Don't you want something smaller?' suggested the Troll.

'A cow's fine,' said Tai. 'She can eat the grass in Mrs Griffiths' garden.'

The man with the microphone kept shouting.
The Troll thought he saw his Aunt on the far side of the crowd.
He waved across to her.

'AUNT SENNI!'

he shouted.

'SOLD...
to the big fellow
at the back,'
announced the man with
the microphone.

The men in hats turned to stare at the Troll.
The Troll smiled and they quickly turned away.

'You've bought a cow,' said Tai.
The black and white cow smiled at the Troll.
**'That'll be three hundred pounds for
the Friesian cow,'** said the auctioneer.

Tai pulled out his pockets. He had twenty-six pence, a world cup medal and a bottle top.

The Troll had a bag of beans, a ball of string and five gold coins.

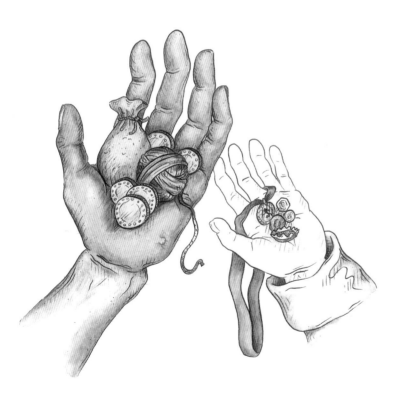

The auctioneer settled for the gold coins and the bottle top.

As the Troll paid the man Aunt Senni arrived.
She was as big as the Troll and even hairier.
'I didn't know you were going into farming, Tremorfa!'
she exclaimed. Her voice boomed around the ring.
'I wasn't,' replied the Troll.

The black and white cow waddled up to Tai and licked his face.
'How do we get her home?' asked Tai.
'In the car of course,' replied the Troll.

They led the cow back to the car and tried pushing her into the back seat.
She didn't want to get in at first but eventually with Aunt Senni pulling one end
and the Troll pushing the other she was squeezed in.

Her head stuck out one side and her tail the other
but she seemed to enjoy the ride home.

The cow rather liked Mrs Griffiths' garden.
The grass was very long and Dai and Slug often
threw her apples from the railway line.